A CLIPPER STREET STORY

ALL I EVER ASK...

Bernard Ashley

Illustrated by Judith Lawton

ORCHARD BOOKS

ORCHARD BOOKS
96 Leonard Street, London EC2A 4RH
Orchard Books Australia
14 Mars Road, Lane Cove, NSW 2066
ISBN 1 85213 864 5
First published in Great Britain 1989
First paperback publication 1996
Text copyright © Bernard Ashley 1989
Illustrations copyright © Judith Lawton 1996
A CIP catalogue record for this book is available from the British Library.
Printed in Great Britain

ALL I EVER
ASK...

Other Clipper Street stories are:

CALLING FOR SAM

TALLER THAN BEFORE

SALLY CINDERELLA

Contents

Chapter One

It was going to be great, really something for a change. The first time ever, and Billy couldn't wait. He'd been excited from the minute his mother had first said it, the minute she'd first said it like that.

"All I ever ask is..." That was the usual. "All I ever ask is..." and then she'd go on about what she never got. A bit of peace. Just one day without them quarrelling—just one. A couple of beds made. Five minutes doing as they were told. It was always the same old song, and it seemed as if Billy had been hearing it for as long as he'd heard voices.

But suddenly, tonight, she'd changed the tune. Tonight she'd come in from cleaning round at the school, got their tea and while she washed up and he dried and Sandra put away, she'd told them.

"Listen, you two, Friday's *my* night. Just for once I'm going to have a bit of fun."

Fun? That seemed odd to Billy, a mother wanting fun. If he'd had a million pounds to buy her a present he wouldn't have spent any of it on fun.

And Sandra was frowning, too. Was it something special on the telly she wanted to watch? One of those old singers she liked?

"No, you can keep your telly. It's none of that. This is something I haven't done for years. I'm treating myself. I'm going out..."

Sandra's eyes went narrow. Billy's went wide. After their father had gone off she'd only been out just the once, with an uncle.

"Going out? Where?"

"Out of this house for five minutes. I don't ask for much, but I reckon I'm in line for five minutes' fun…"

Which sounded just like a ride on the dodgems, but Billy guessed it had to be something different to that.

"If I can trust you…"

They both started nodding like puppets.

"You're old enough to be left, Sandra," she said. "Just for a couple of hours. And you can look after Billy. Girls your age baby-sit for other people down the street..."

"*Baby*-sit?" Billy didn't like the sound of that: but Sandra shut him up with a lightning wink. There'd be fun in this for all of them, it said.

"We'll be all right, Mum. Won't we, Billy?"

"Yeah," Billy joined in, "you go out on the tiles!"

"Here! I'm not your cat. But it should be nice..." She smiled to herself in the sink, went a shade red. "It's a firm's dinner-and-dance down at the *Embassy*..."

"Who with? Uncle Steve? That Brian...?"

Mrs Drew shook her head, sounded all off-hand. "Oh, never you mind. Well, just a friend. His name's...Tony..."

"Whoa-oh-oah!" Sandra whooped. "*Tony!*"

"And you can leave that out!"

"Yeah, shut up!" Billy said. But his voice had come out like someone else's. Because his dad's name was *Ken*; and he'd just wondered...just for a second. Well, you never knew, did you? People did get together again...

Chapter Two

There wasn't going to be any mucking about. When she went out at seven they were both going to be ready for bed: in their pyjamas and fed and washed and ready to go up, with no need to light the stove or use any matches. The back door would be double-bolted and all the windows locked. All they had to do was lock the front door behind her.

"And you get to bed before the News," she told them. "I'm not going to be *that* late…"

Billy pulled a face: but Sandra kept hers straight.

"And you can leave the front room tidy, in

case we come back here for a coffee ..."

"Whoa-oh-whoa!" Sandra couldn't help it—and so she got her legs smacked as she was chased halfway up the stairs.

"You know I like the place nice! What the devil's the matter with you, you stupid girl? I won't go if you're going to be *stupid*!"

But Billy managed to take the red off her face. It'd be all right, he told her. They'd be sensible. And he wouldn't drop any crisps or peanuts on the floor: if he did he'd get them up.

Their mother had a bang about in the kitchen. But she was humming, and she put a tape on while the pre-wash got done. Which was good news. Because Billy had decided that he really wanted her to go. For her sake, sure, but for his own as well. It could be a good night, the Friday coming. He'd been thinking about it, and he'd made up his mind.

He knew Sandra. She'd go up and have the stereo on in her room without the head-phones, deafen everyone and dance to herself in the wardrobe mirror. That's what she got up to when their mum was out shopping.

Him—he had different ideas. For him it was going to be do-as-you-please for a whole evening: with no one to go on about how many Cokes he had, or keep a check on the minutes in between them, or stop him watching the horror film, or keep on about where he put his feet, or tick him off when he burped. But especially no one to stop him watching that film: *The Blood of Dr Syn*... Some of the kids had been talking about it in school, the ones who watched everything, and it sounded really scary: all the *big* kids were going to see *Dr Syn* on Friday night ...

Chapter Three

Their mother did look nice. Billy realised he'd never thought of her as being pretty, what with her being his mother. But when she came down from her bedroom Sandra whistled and he nearly swallowed his chewing gum. She hadn't overdone it, but she still looked like someone off a Hollywood film. She wore a pink top a bit low, scattered with little shiny pearls, and her arms were bare. Her trousers were black silk, her heels were high; and her toes definitely looked like someone else's. Her hair glistened in a special curly style, and her face was made-up like a

model's—although she tried to keep it
straight, as if she wasn't really anything out of
the ordinary.

But, "Whoa-oh..." Sandra opened her mouth and nearly said it.

"All right, you children?" Mrs Drew tried to sound very business-like. "There's peanuts and Coke in the kitchen." But her voice came from a long way off, it wasn't quite hers. And her eyes didn't settle on anything the way they normally did. No, she wasn't quite with them.

"Now you behave yourselves, you two, and no bother, you hear? If there's anything up, really up, like Nan on the phone not well, I've left the number where I'll be..."

"Or dial 999," said Billy, trying to show how sensible he could be.

"No! Help Us! Only 999 if it's life or death! Here, are you two sure you're going to be all right?"

Sandra gave a killer of a stare at Billy.

"'Course we will. Go on, Mum, or he'll

think you've stood him up…"

"He'd better not!" Mrs Drew took a last look in the hall mirror, just stared, waited while Sandra held the front door open.

"Have a good time."

"Oooh! I'm not sure…" She was very nervous.

"Ta-ta, Mum."

"Oooh! And be *good*!"

Chapter Four

She'd gone. Her shoes clacked away down the street till they couldn't be heard any more. Sandra and Billy looked at one another. And looked, and looked, stood as still as chess pieces and looked, Billy waiting for Sandra to move and Sandra waiting for Billy. Him waiting for her to go upstairs; and her waiting for him to do the same thing.

"Clear off, Billy! Go on, clear off out of the way..." Sandra ran into the front room and went over to the window. She looked out, checking down the road; and ran back to the hall to grab up the phone.

"Go on, Billy! Find something to do up in your own room." She pushed at the numbers.

"Eh?"

"You heard!"

Billy slumped against the wall, stayed there and watched her face change as somebody answered.

"That you, Kell?... Yeah, she's gone. Didn't half look nice. Anyhow, you comin' over?" She twisted round and stared hard at Billy. "Billy's going up to bed."

Billy came off the wall. So that was it! Because he was in his pyjamas and ready for bed, she thought he was going there! And she'd had this plan to get Kelly round here all the time. Even as the cheat of it pumped his heart faster, off came her dressing gown and there she was still in her blouse and long shorts.

"You rotten..." Billy started. But Sandra had thrown her dressing gown halfway up the stairs and was telling him... "Listen, you,

Kelly's coming round with some videos. So you can make yourself scarce, OK? Get some toys out in your room..."

But Billy's mouth was set, too. His eyes could rivet with a stare as hard as anyone's. "Get lost! Get your own toys out. I'm having the telly. Mum never said you could have anyone round..."

"And she never said you could watch what *you* want to watch. Ten o'clock she said..."

"I'm telling her. She never said Kelly could come..."

"And she never said you could watch horror!" Eyeball into eyeball they stared. "We're not stopping you watching our videos till ten o'clock; but you haven't got to make any noise..."

"What, *music*?"

"Or clear off upstairs. I'm s'posed to be looking after you. Mum won't mind Kelly

coming round to help me baby-sit."

"*Baby-sit*?!" That was it! Billy had heard that once too often, and now he gave in to his temper. He threw the phone book at her. "I'm not a baby!" It missed, so he followed it with Thompson's Directory.

Which Sandra caught. "No? Look at you! Chucking things!"

Yellow Pages went next and broke its back against the door jamb.

"So it's up to you, Sunshine!" Like a busy hostess, Sandra scooped up the phone books and hurried through to the kitchen. While Billy, just about holding back the tears, made a sign at her, pulled a hateful face, and thumped like thunder up the stairs.

Chapter Five

He wanted to kick the walls of his room in his rage. He'd told everyone in the playground about him being allowed to see *The Blood of Dr Syn*, said how he'd let the unlucky ones know what it was all about.

Now he'd look a little liar, wouldn't he? How could he tell them that he'd not been allowed at all...and by his baby-sitter sister? He ground his teeth, put on the face he twisted to frighten the Infants. Well, one thing was sure: he wasn't going to sit up here: he wasn't going to be some prisoner...

He looked outside. It was still light.

Then, blow keeping the back door locked and bolted—he was going in the garden with his football. He'd got to kick something!

Sandra took no notice. All she seemed worried about was him keeping out of her way. She was busy in the front room putting low lights on like a disco, sorting out the video; and she didn't hear him fighting with the bolts and getting out there with his ball.

Being a bit wise, he didn't go out on the grass where he'd be seen from next door. He kicked his ball up under the back room window on the concrete path. It wasn't all that warm in his pyjamas and the wind was getting up, shifting the crunchy grains of sand the council workmen had left, whipping fine waves of it underfoot. But he could cope with that, he was steady on his trainers. With a smack he cracked the ball against the brickwork, got one good kick out of his system and

went into dribbling skills and some of the
wall passes Sam next door had been teaching
him. He almost enjoyed it: and only when he
could hardly see what he was doing in the
dark did he let himself get driven in by the
cold wind that had gone on blowing.

He bolted the back door behind him, made as much noise as he wanted. Let her know he was boss of himself. But still Sandra didn't seem to care, so he went through into the front room to poke his nose. And then he could see why she wasn't bothering about him. Kelly had already come; and there they were, the two of them, lounging back on the settee trying to look all cool, as if they shared some flat.

"What do you want?" But Sandra hardly even bothered to look round. She was too busy clicking her fingers at some smarmy-haired singer on the video who was posing into the camera.

"Erk! How long's this thing last?"

"Till you're well asleep!"

"Oh, yeah?" Billy looked at the video clock. His film would be on in two hours. He looked at the pile of videos Kelly had brought: enough to last a week.

"My film's on at ten o'clock. I want the telly then, you know." He made it sound very definite; he wouldn't take Sandra saying no.

"No way!"

"You! I said ..."

But Sandra only grabbed the remote control and upped the sound, made the cat sit up in his basket, deafened her ears to Billy.

"Right!" He slammed the door, banged up

the stairs. Right! They wanted a war, then they could have one. And he suddenly found himself smiling a grim smile—because what stupid Sandra had just done had given him an idea. They wanted the telly, well they could have it. And a lot of good it'd do them—the way he was going to leave it. After the stroke he was going to pull...

Chapter Six

Billy made his plans carefully. He was going to have to know exactly what moves he would make—and be sure to make them quickly when the time came. There wouldn't be any second chances. Quietly, he went over everything in his mind. For a few minutes he laid on his bed and pictured the whole thing. He didn't want any slip-ups. He closed his eyes, squinted at the pictures in his head.

And shot his eyes open again in a wild scare as a sudden gust of wind rattled at his window like the shaking of a giant hand.

Wow! He pulled the curtains and looked

out, knew it was only the wind, but just had to be sure… There was nothing there, of course: no hand on the frame, no face at the glass. But he'd rather be downstairs, all the same. And, anyway, now was the time, if he was going to give his plan a chance to work; if he was going to have something to do a deal with.

Quietly, he opened all the doors upstairs, found what he wanted in Sandra's room, and went down to where the loud music was com-

ing from. Call that good? he thought. It was rubbish. It had nothing on a proper film like *The Blood of Dr Syn*!

Outside the front room he waited for a couple of seconds, wiped the smile off his face as best he could, and then walked in. As pleasant as you like. Mr Nice Guy.

"Wotcha!" He stroked the cat in his basket, sat down as if he meant to stay. "I quite like this one…" The video was flashing out another rotten tune, danced-to by stupid puppets.

He got a sharp look from Kelly; a suspicious one from Sandra. But they soon went back to the screen, and, squinting from the corners of his eyes, Billy was pleased to see that everything was exactly as he wanted.

He sat back, looked relaxed with his head and his neck and his arms. His legs were tense, though, and all ready to go.

Now. One, two, three... With a sudden spring he threw himself forward, dived for the remote control on Sandra's knee and scooped it up. In the same burst of movement he killed the lights at the door, and, twisting as he ran, pointed the control at the set and pressed his thumb down hard on the stand-by button.

The room went dark—and silent, if you didn't count the screams and shouts coming from Sandra and her friend.

"Come back here!"

"You rotten little…!"

For a second or so it was all chaos, stumbles, and swearing until some light was spilled when the door opened and Billy could be seen with the black thing in his hand, legging it for the stairs.

Chapter Seven

"Come back! Come back, you! Give it here!" Sandra was only ever a grab behind.

"Enjoy your videos! If you can hear 'em!" But Billy knew they couldn't. There was no sound control actually on the set. There was a button to get the channel back but the sound would be too low. You always needed the remote control to turn it up. And Billy had grabbed it... Now he ran upstairs and banged into his mother's bedroom, slammed the door and locked it from the inside.

Only a breath behind him, Sandra started pounding on its panels. "Let me in! You

creep! I'm gonna murder you, Billy! I'm gonna do you for this!"

Billy said nothing, just waited. It took her three or four minutes to quieten down, but in the end she was ready to listen.

"You got another hour and a half," he told her through the door. "You let me have my film when it comes on an' you can have another hour and a half of your stupid videos first ..."

Sandra swore. But Kelly, behind her,

helped her to see some sort of sense in the bargain. "Say yes," she whispered. "Do what he says. We'll think of something…"

Not sure, Sandra turned back and looked at the door with hatred, as if the door were Billy. Then, "All right," she muttered. "Creep! Come out. We'll do a deal…"

"Promise?"

"Yes! Come on, hurry up, you're wasting *our* time."

Billy's head came round the slowly opened door; the winner, but still not too sure.

"You can look where you like in there," he stood back and told them. "You won't get the remote till you promise."

"I did promise."

"Not *on your mother's death bed*."

Sandra swallowed, looked in at her mother's bed. It was pink and lacy and the thought of it being anything else made her shudder. But then so did the thought of going through her mother's private cupboards and drawers for the remote control. She looked at Kelly, who nodded at her solemnly.

"On my mother's death bed," Sandra said, the words like dry biscuits in her mouth.

"Right!" said Billy. "You said it. Well, the thing's not here." From behind his back he pulled Sandra's pocket calculator, the decoy which had drawn them upstairs after him. He gave it to her with a little nod of

thanks. "The real one's down in the cat basket." He laughed, more than full of himself.
"I bet he's laid on it and changed your rotten
video over already…"

Chapter Eight

They left him to *The Blood of Dr Syn*: at least, they left him to the start of it. He'd kept his bargain and let them watch their videos, so they kept theirs. Anyway, when he stopped watching it would be all his own choice...

On his own, he swallowed the warning about how frightening it would be, how unsuitable it was for nervous people; and with a freeze of fright prickling across the skin of his arms, he sat with the light full on and stared through the opening scenes. It was about smuggling and ghosts and fear, out on the Romney Marshes—and from the start the creepy music and the dark night of the film made sure he kept an eye on the curtains, and on the door of the front room. He kidded himself he was really enjoying it, all the close-ups of evil, all the deaths: but he was glad now that Sandra was in the house, and very pleased that the bolts were on the doors. Like that, he reckoned he could just about cope with what he was watching. What if he

did have to half close his eyes and his fingers were ready to block his ears? Even gown-ups did that, didn't they? No, he *wasn't* going to switch the thing off and say it was all rubbish and go to bed, like some kids would. Not him. Not yet...

Not until the lights suddenly went out— and just as the face of Dr Syn was staring right at him, coming for him through the fog;

and just as a devilish wail and a deathly cackle started coming at him from the other side of the front room door.

He screamed. The cat shot up and arched its back. "Shut up! Don't do that!" It was only Sandra and Kelly, he knew, but it was sudden and horrible: and all at once he was scared stiff, even of them.

As the door burst open he threw himself out of his chair to face the danger. And in they came, the first one under a sheet drawn tight and death-like round the head; the other in an old buttoned-up black coat and a stocking mask. But he couldn't see their eyes as they came for him with their bony, clawing fingers and their graveyard voices—and suddenly they weren't Sandra and Kelly at all any more but these frightening creatures they'd invented.

"Tear out his heart and eat it!"

"Suck the juice from his bones!"

They sounded as if they meant it: as if they could do it.

"Get away! Leave me alone! I'm telling Mum!"

But the first one only laughed, high and shrill. "You will never see your mother ever again!"

And still they came at him, bent and grab-
bing, less and less human as they got taken
over by what they were doing.

"Oooooh! Aaaaah! Ha, ha, ha, ha, ha,
ha!" The sheet suddenly turned on the black
coat. The black coat screamed. "Ha, ha, ha,
ha, ha!" And Billy darted for the door, for his
life, the film forgotten, his heart pounding in

its panic. "Get away! Stop it!" He didn't even dare to pull the sheet from off the head for fear of what he'd see. He ran from the front room into the back, tried to slam the door on them. But they were there, pursuing, coming at him.

The ghost raised its arm. "Come, boy, give yourself to me..."

The arms were coming to embrace him. No! A cuddle from that would kill! And he was trapped. He turned and ran to the window, any escape... But as his hands went clutching at the curtains the wind hit the house as it had before and the window rattled like a demon going at it.

Their three screams were as one. Their fright made sticks of their backs. Hair stood on end, hard as pins. Their voices were all their own again as the three of them clutched at each other in terror: the ghost, the ghoulie,

and the horror film addict. They gripped hard, pinched skin and didn't feel it as they fell silent for a second. Only to hit the ceiling with their hearts when a new noise came from out at the back.

Something which sounded like the stealthy crunch of footsteps on the sandy path...

Chapter Nine

Three hearts almost stopped. Breathing was held back as the crunch came again from somewhere very near the back window. But this time, instead of screaming at the wind they stood in a rigid ring of real and silent fear. There was someone outside. Someone who shouldn't be there…

Somehow Sandra fought herself free and tore the sheet from over her head. Kelly's fingers ripped at the long line of buttons. Their cheeks felt frozen. The only sound now came from throats which were swallowing and gulping. This was real—and Billy had never felt so frightened in all his life, his stomach one ache of terror.

"I'm off!" Kelly yelled, running for the door. "I'm going home, out of here…"

All Sandra and Billy could do was hug each other tighter and stare at the curtains. While, crunch, crunch, came the stealthy sound again. *Could he see in? Could he hear what they were saying?*

Not waiting to know, Kelly had gone: ignored her bag, left her videos, run past Dr Syn without a look: and almost leapt out of her skin as she'd thrown open the front door.

A tall man was standing there; a tall man with a beard; Sam Roberts from next door, with his girlfriend behind him.

"You all right?" he asked. He put a hand on Kelly's shoulder, stopped her from running into the road. He looked beyond her down the hall to where Sandra and Billy were still huddled and shaking.

"What's going on?" He was half looking for their mother. "I'm not one for banging on the wall, but it sounds like murder's going off in here."

Billy ran up to him: his friend, the man who coached him at football. "Mum's out. And there's a bloke outside in our garden…"

"Is there?" Sam came in, asked his girl-friend to be ready by the phone, and went boldly through into the kitchen. "You seen him?"

"Heard him."

"Not the wind?"

"No, footsteps!"

"Then I'll have him!" In one quick, big movement Sam slid the bolt aside and turned the key open in the lock. "Stand back!" he said. And out he went.

Chapter Ten

The garden was empty. There wasn't a sign of anyone anywhere, just the wind whipping at the leaves and grass. Televisions and radios could be heard further down the street. Normal life. A bit bolder now, Billy and Sandra followed him out.

"Wonder if he's gone over?" Sam was up on the fence, looking into his own garden; and Billy was up on the other fence, looking over into next door down's. And still there was no sign of anyone.

"We'll give the police a bell," Sam said. "We don't want nothing like this starting round here…" Eyes all about him still, he led the way indoors again; got near to the back door—and suddenly stopped. There was no one there but he stopped, and he stood facing the window through which they'd heard the sound.

"Come here," he said to the others. They did as he said, tiptoed up and stood alongside him, facing the way he was facing. "Now, listen…" He put a finger to his lips.

They listened. And they looked. And as the wind blew they saw and they heard— Billy's plastic football rolling slowly over the sand, backwards and forwards in the enclosed space; crunching stealthily, just like footsteps.

"There's your man!" Sam said. "Mr Ball!" And with a hard ruffle of Billy's hair, he went. Just stopped at the front door to ask one question.

"Where *is* your mum?" he wanted to know.

"Down the *Embassy*. She won't be long."

If Sam had thoughts about that he didn't share them.

"You won't…like…tell her how scared we got, will you?" Billy asked.

"Nor the racket you made?" He stared from one to the other of them. "Depends whether you give me and Linda a bit of peace from now on…" He looked at his girlfriend who was down by the front gate.

"Oh, we will. Honest. Ta. Thanks, Sam"

"Yeah, thanks very much," Sandra added. "Sorry …"

Chapter Eleven

They made sure they were in bed when their mother came in. Everywhere was tidy, all the washing up was done, there wasn't a crisp or a peanut on the floor, and not even a ring-pull from a can.

Her hair had been ruined by the wind, and she was on her own.

"Have a good time?" Sandra called down.

"Yeah, it was all right…"

They came down the stairs to see her.

"It wasn't all that special, really. But it was a night out…" She pulled off her shoes, rubbed her toes. "How about you?

Everything all right here, was it?"

"Yeah!"

"Great! No problems!"

They said it quickly and loudly, but she didn't seem to notice.

"No arguments? No one banging on the wall?"

They shook their heads.

"That's good," she said. "Then I can do it again some time if I want to…"

"Sure…"

"Yeah…"

"You know, that's all I ever ask," she said. "Just a little bit of being nice to one another, brother and sister. It makes a real difference, a little bit of co-operation…"